Welcome to your loc

We love to help you and

Let's see who is here to greet;

so many animals to meet!

Bunny's first; she rang the bell.

Let us help her feel well!

We must treat her without stopping,

so she can get back to hopping!

Dr. Chuck! Dr. Chuck!

I cannot hear you, Dr. Chuck!

What did you say? I cannot hear!

I think that I have hurt my ears!

Let me look inside
your ear;
I think I see the
problem here.

There is something
that I see;
a carrot where it
should not be!

Please do not put things in your ear.

That's not for eating;

it's where you hear!

I think that you will find relief

if you only eat carrots with your teeth!

Frog, my friend, welcome in;
you're my favorite amphibian!
You look dried up (you should be wetter).
How can we help you feel better?

Thank you, just as you can tell,
you see I am not feeling well.

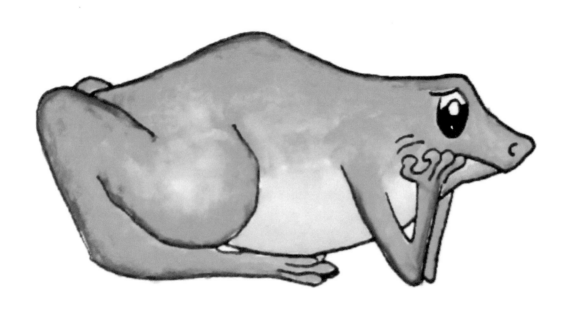

This has been hard for me a tid bit;
I hiccup when I try to ribbit!

Oh no, my friend! That does sound bad; it sounds just like hiccups I've had!

How sad to see a healthy frog sounding like a pollywog.

I have good news, though,
they will not last!
These hiccups should
go away fast!

And then you can jump
        and croak
and play with other froggy folk!

Here is Turtle in her shell;

let's make sure she is feeling well!

She never needs a bed to sleep in;

she has her shell for counting sheep in!

Dr. Chuck, as you can see,

I have lost my favorite knee!

I need to use this knee to kneel,

but this knee I cannot feel!

Turtle you will
soon be well;
your knee is still
inside your shell!

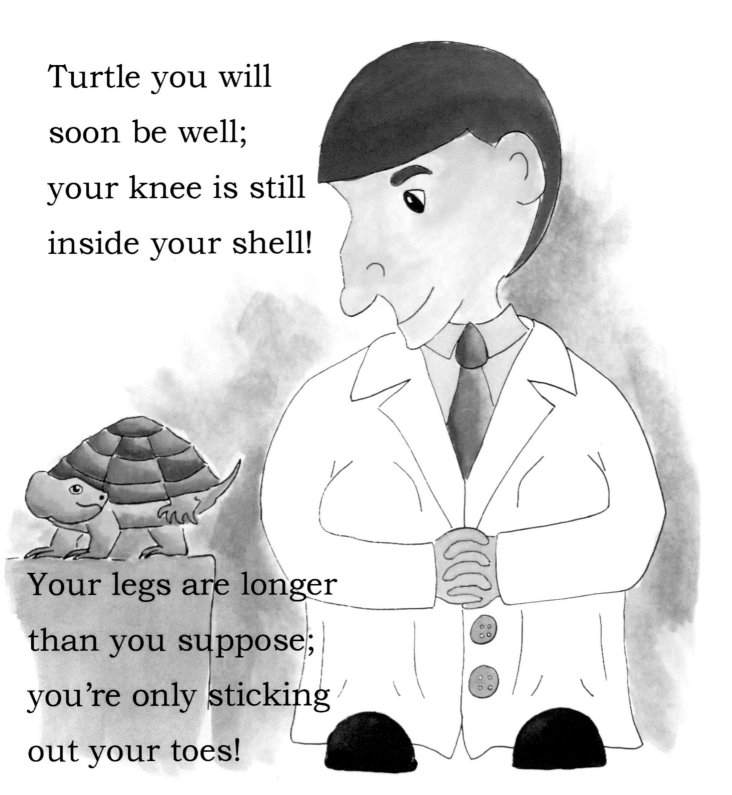

Your legs are longer
than you suppose;
you're only sticking
out your toes!

Here's our friend with ruffled feather;

let us see how we can help her!

She hasn't very far to go;

she came from just across the road!

My belly is not feeling well;
it has been this way for a spell.

It's larger than it was before,
and I worry what's in store!

Something's going on in there,
but I cannot tell quite
where!

There are these feathers
in the way;
we can see through
with an X-ray!

My Chicken friend, you can rest easy.

Soon you will

not be so queasy!

But please

sit down!

Right here

I beg!

You are about to lay an egg!

Puppy's walking in the door;

let's find out what he's here for!

Though his ears are hanging low,

his tail's wagging to and fro!

I don't have very much to say;
I'm just here for my shots today!

I need to get them, so do you,
so I feel good tomorrow too!

It's nice to see you here again;
I'm glad you're feeling
well my friend!

Just one quick shot, then on your way,
so you don't get sick some other day!

A shot is not
so bad to get,
although it stings
(a little bit).

Be brave a second, just for a beat,
and afterwards you get a treat!

Hedgehog is our last patient today,

I wonder what he has to say.

Though full of quills, we give him love,

but we may need to wear a glove!

Dr. Chuck, what's going on?
I'm shivering all day long!

Ah-Choo!

I cannot stop this running nose,
and when I sneeze I poke my toes!

My hedgehog friend,
this may sound silly,
but your house is much
too chilly!

You must be in
a warmer state,
or you will start
to hibernate!

A hedgehog should be warm and cozy,
your cheeks should not turn so rosy!

Turn up the heat, stay under the covers,
and then, my friend, you will recover!

Thank you for your help today;
our animals are feeling great!

Taking care of all these pets
is why I love to be a vet!

45457670R00017

Made in the USA
Middletown, DE
04 July 2017

Like us on Facebook @DrChuckBooks
for the latest updates!

And visit us at Society6 for art and prints of
your favorite animals!

society6.com/drchuck

ISBN 9781548076917

90000

9 781548 076917